M is for Monster

A Fantastic Creatures Alphabet

Written by J. Patrick Lewis and Illustrated by Gerald Kelley

A a

In Inuit legend, Amarok is an enormous lone wolf that stalks any hunter foolish enough to go out after dark.

When the earliest Inuit people crossed the Bering land bridge from the Old World to the New thousands of years ago, they must have been well acquainted with the "dire wolf" (*Canis dirus*), which lived from 1.8 million to about 10,000 years ago. It was not the ancestor of any wolf today. But people who look for the origins of the mysterious Amarok believe the dire wolf just may be a long-lost descendant.

Was he five feet long and two hundred pounds, as some people claim? Did he savagely carry off dogs and sheep? If he was frightening, as the Inuit believed, he was also a good omen. When the caribou population grew too large, Amorak, so it was thought, arrived to kill the weak and dying animals so that the herd could become healthy again, and the hunt could go on.

But as Inuit populations diminish, the Amarok myth may gradually die out as well.

A is for Amarok

The Inuit were afraid of Amarok,
    a wicked wolf that pounced to the attack.
And some who dared the forest of the night
    unluckily would not be coming back.

Baba Yaga is a monstrous, supernatural old witch with gruesome iron teeth who flies through the air on a mortar with a pestle as her steering wheel. (Mortars and pestles, used for grinding grain into flour, were very common in Russia long ago.) Her house is strange beyond belief. The front door key-hole looks like a mouth with sharp fangs. Standing on chicken-legs, the hut whirls around constantly. The fence is made of skulls and bones.

In English, *Baba Yaga* (pronounced Ya-GA) means Granny Yaga. Her nose is so long it bumps against the ceiling when she snores. She kidnaps children, then eats them, even though Boney Legs (her other nickname) is as skinny as a pole. Or, if she sees them coming, she drops her jaw, huge as a cave, and swallows them whole.

Enormously popular in cartoons, Baba Yaga is a household word in Russian culture. She also appears in novels, television shows, and films. Despite her fierce reputation, she is occasionally portrayed as a helpful side-kick to the hero of the story.

B b

B is for Baba Yaga
"Come, my pretty,
let me see
how delicious you will be
with my raspberry jam and tea!"

A centaur is a member of a race of creatures whose lower body is that of a horse, but with a human upper body where the horse's neck would be. One of the most fascinating creatures of Greek mythology, centaurs are said to live in mountain caves. With rocks and rough tree branches, these savages hunt for wild animals. With few exceptions, they are known mostly as aggressive and lawless beings.

The origins of the centaur are claimed by many cultures. The Aztecs, who had never seen men on horseback, were at first convinced that the newly arrived Spanish soldiers were a strange breed of half-man, half-horse. Horse taming in the steppes of Central Asia, still prevalent today, also fueled centaur speculation.

Centaurs can be seen on Greek pottery and well-known sculptures in the Old World, and they appear in C.S. Lewis's *The Chronicles of Narnia* and also in J.K. Rowling's Harry Potter series, where they were said to live in the Forbidden Forest next door to Hogwarts School of Witchcraft and Wizardry.

C is for Centaur

Who says there's nothing
new under the sun?
A horse and man?
Here's two in one!

D d

D is for Dragon

I am Dragon,
 one who seeks and slays
with smoke and fire.
 They call me Blaze.

Almost every culture has its own favorite dragon. No matter where they were allegedly spotted or were believed to be hiding —especially in Japan, China, and Greece— these flame-belching giants were known for their huge appetites, consisting mainly of unwary livestock or ill-fated humans.

Western (European) dragons possess wings; Eastern (Chinese) dragons are serpentine. The dragonlike creature that lacks front legs is called a wyvern. Dragons can breathe fire and lay eggs, and they have scales or feathers, as well as enormous tails. Their name means "to see clearly" and they could sometimes be taught to guard valuable property, such as castles, princesses, even empires.

In the East, dragons are just as often respected as feared. They are connected to nature, the universe, and religion. The very idea of a dragon may have first originated with Nile crocodiles, whale skeletons, or other fossil finds. Early mapmakers, ignorant of many unexplored areas in the world, would often mark their maps by simply writing (in Latin), "Here be dragons."

E is for Elf

An elf I am,
    gentle as a lamb,
    but in days gone by,
        horrid was I.

Ee

Small in size, an elf is a supernatural being that lives in forests, rocks, springs, and wells, and can appear at will. These sprites are thought to have magical powers that can help or hurt humans.

In Scandinavian folklore, they can be stunningly beautiful females, often dressed in white. (*Elf* means "white one" in Latin.) But they can also be nasty creatures, capable of harming livestock or dancing a man to death. At night or on misty mornings, they might be seen dancing in circles on a lakeshore. If you watch them for what seems to be just a few hours, several years will have passed in real time.

In England and Scotland, elves evolved into brownies and hobgoblins, kind or sinister, depending upon the teller of the tale. Now, of course, probably because of their holiday association as Santa's helpers with pointy ears and charming personalities, elves are considered, almost universally, affectionate creatures.

The legend of Frankenstein is a story about a monstrous creature that was created from a failed scientific experiment. The English summer of 1816 was particularly rainy and gloomy. So Mary Wollstonecraft Shelley (1797–1851), aged 18, and her friend, later her husband, the poet Percy Bysshe Shelley, went to Switzerland to visit another great poet, Lord George Gordon Byron. One evening, Byron suggested that each of them write a ghost story.

Mary Shelley's story involved a young doctor, Victor Frankenstein, who hoped to design a beautiful and intelligent creature. Instead, the fiend was a frightening, eight-foot-tall giant. (By the way, the monster was never given a name in Ms. Shelley's book, but over time he assumed the doctor's name.)

The poor monster became so lonely that he told Dr. Frankenstein, "You are my creator, but I am your master!" He demanded that the doctor create a mate for him. In the end, this tale, like much of world literature, centers on the basic conflict of good vs. evil. It's a fascinating story with many surprising twists and turns, but you can read it yourself. Mary Shelley's masterpiece is as close as your library.

F is for Frankenstein

Science and progress
        might move right along,
but I'm living proof
        that things can go wrong!

Ff

G g

A gargoyle is a sculpture made of stone and attached to a building (often a church or cathedral) to make certain that rainwater runs beyond the side and does not eat away the mortar. But that is not the first thing people think of when they see these hideous granite monsters.

In French, *gargouille* means "gullet" or "throat," perhaps because of the gurgling water sound it makes from the runoff. It has the added feature of protecting against evil spirits. Yet religious leaders often used these faces to frighten people into attending church services. A French legend claims that St. Romain saved the city of Rouen from a monster called Gargouille, a bat-winged, fire-breathing dragon. Accounts vary, but one telling suggests that when the beast was captured and burned, its head and neck resisted the flames because of its own internal fire. Mounted on the wall of a newly built church, the head then served to protect the building and its parishioners.

The European gargoyles today have the heads of lions, dogs, monkeys, snakes, wolves, eagles, goats, or mythical creatures.

G is for Gargoyle

The face on the face
of a building? That's me.
Granite carved into
monstrosity!

A winged legend, the hippogriff has the back legs of a horse, but the head and body of a griffin (also spelled griffon or gryphon). Remember Buckbeak, later renamed Witherwings? He was the hippogriff in the Harry Potter series.

Hippogriffs are extremely fast and able to fly around the world. In times past they were often ridden by knights, magicians, and heroes of old. The average hippogriff is nine feet long, has a twenty-foot wingspan, and weighs as much as a water buffalo. Since they are omnivores (they will eat any-thing!), they aren't very picky. Hippogriffs will eat a tulip as fast as a turnip. Or a human as easily as a chicken!

H h

H is for Hippogriff

Half an eagle, half a horse,
    I'm all hippogriff, of course.
Back end tail, front end beak;
    put together make me *s-t-r-e-a-k!*

I is for Imp

An imp is incredibly clever,
  outrageously naughty and wild;
  a bit like your next-door neighbor's
  small but IMPossible child!

You may not hear the word "imp" much anymore, but sometimes parents would call their children imps if they were being impolite. An imp, meaning small devil—an offshoot of Satan— is a favorite character in mythology. Much like fairies, with which they are often compared, imps are very small homely creatures full of nervous energy. In some cultures, they are thought to work side by side with witches as their spies.

In German folklore these little folk are considered lesser demons, but demons aren't always bad. Naughty maybe, but not downright evil. Imps tend to be ornery. They will give people the wrong directions, pull chairs out from under them, or tell little white lies. Like fairies, these hooligans have a fondness for playing pranks. Despite their misbehavior, they seem to crave human attention and affection. But even then, these odd creatures keep up their practical jokes.

Ii

J is for Jersey Devil

An American monster,
spotted by loads
of people near backyards,
in forests, on roads.

J j

WELCOME TO New Jersey

Imagine a U.S. state having its own legendary creature! Some folks claim to have seen the "Jersey Devil" in the remote Pine Barrens of southern New Jersey. What does it look like? Who can say for sure? Many agree that it walks on two feet, or rather hooves, has batlike wings, a forked tail, and a piercing screech.

The legend started in 1735 when a woman known as Mother Leeds, possibly a witch, was giving birth to her thirteenth child. Not wanting the burden of another child, Mother Leeds begged the devil to take it. And so he did. Upon its birth, the grotesque creature began beating everyone in the room with its tail, including Mrs. Leeds, before screaming and vanishing into a storm. Ever since, claims of destroyed crops and livestock, poisoned pools and creeks have been blamed on the Jersey Devil.

There have been numerous alleged sightings, but no photographs. Whether there is any truth to the myth, the Jersey Devil has become the state's cultural symbol, and a professional hockey team bears its name.

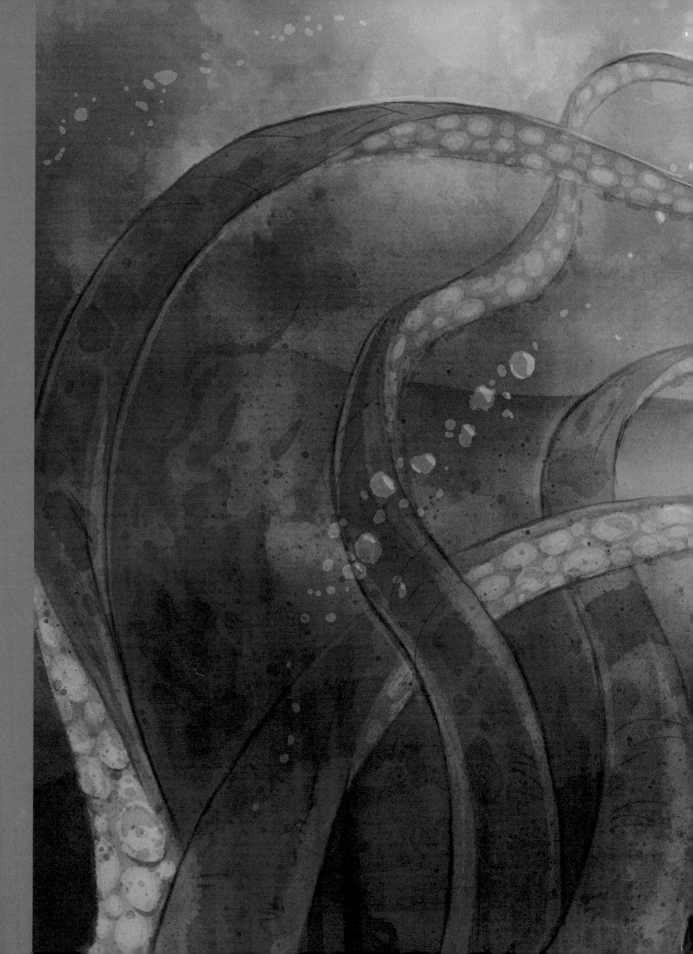

As sea monsters go, first prize belongs to the legendary Kraken, said to dwell off the coasts of Iceland and Norway. Most likely a sailor's tall tale from centuries ago, today the Kraken is represented in films, literature, video games, and even on postage stamps.

The word *Kraken* means "octopus" in German, and its appearance and characteristics tell you why it earned that name. Fishermen willing to risk it fished directly over the location of a Kraken spotting because that's where fishing was thought to be the best. But once the monster has finished its months-long meals of smaller fish on the ocean floor, it rises slowly ... and heaven help the poor sailor who is sitting on the surface. With flailing arms, dreadful nostrils, and an enormous head, the Kraken's whirlpool is alleged to resemble the creation of a new island. Boats are swallowed and fishermen eaten.

There is little doubt that the sea monster is based on something real, either a colossal octopus or, more recently, the notoriously reclusive giant squid.

k
K

K is for Kraken

Of all the legends of the sea,
  sailors and fishermen agree
  (if they lived to tell my tale!),
  I could wrestle shark or whale.

The Loch Ness Monster may have done more to capture the public's imagination than any other monster in history, except perhaps for Bigfoot. Some claim its origins date back to the seventh century, but it was first spotted (allegedly) by Alex Campbell, a part-time journalist in 1933. Nessie, as she is lovingly called by the locals, is said to inhabit Loch (Lake) Ness in the Scottish Highlands.

Photographs of her movements are blurry, sonar soundings are unreliable, and "scientific" evidence of her existence is doubtful. This has not stopped the tall tales that "something" unexplained patrols these waters. That something, so the claim goes, may be a throwback to the plesiosaurs, which died out with the rest of the dinosaurs 65 million years ago.

Variously seen by observers as an elephant, a walrus, an otter, a long-necked seal, a snake, seismic gas—even a gnarled tree—the Loch Ness Monster has also created its share of outright hoaxers, who have tried to cash in on the phenomenon. The only thing we know for certain about Nessie is that she is sure to be with us for a very long time to come.

L l

L is for Loch Ness Monster

Am I fake? Or am I real?
    An enormous monster eel?
The truth is anybody's guess.
    Maybe I'm just clever-
        Ness.

M m

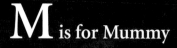

M is for Mummy

Can a daddy
be a mummy?
Who knows
what's wrapped in that suit of clothes?

Mummies have been around for millennia. Various cultures have preserved mummies by covering corpses with lake salt, vinegar, ice, and local concoctions, and then placing them in extreme temperatures. An English word derived from Latin and Persian, *mummy* comes from the word "mummia," which refers to bitumen, a black, tarlike substance.

The oldest-known intentional mummy is a Chilean child dating from about 5000 BC, though Mother Nature has created a mummified human head dating to six thousand years. Over a thousand mummies have been discovered in China, and in Egypt, over a million, but most of them are cats.

Preserving loved ones by mummifying them suggests a strong belief in the afterlife. Often, mummies' coffins were lined with gold or silver, even clothes and toothbrushes to help the dead find an easy path to a new existence.

The first mummies were the Egyptian Pharaohs and their families, but the practice of mummification spread to commoners as well. Of course, they were enthusiastically welcomed in Western popular culture, either for humor or horror. Who doesn't find the idea of the walking dead (corpses come to life) either silly or frightening?

N is for Naiad

Naiad's the name
    that brought her fame
beside a healing stream.
    Or was it all a dream?

N n

In ancient mythology, a naiad is a type of water nymph (mythical girl) who lives near fresh water, such as a fountain, spring, stream, or brook. Beautiful but unpredictable, naiads can also be cruel. In stories, boys and girls coming of age would often give them their youthful curls as a gift.

The name *naiad* comes from the Greek and means "running water." Her very life is bound to her spring, and if it dries up, she will die soon after. Every spring has its own naiad presiding over it. Anyone whose illness is cured by these magical waters knows that the naiad is to thank for the healing.

As daughters of Zeus or other river gods, these nymphs usually live near them. But naiads were also known to fall in love with and sometimes marry mortals. Mythology abounds with tales of naiad–human marriages, but since naiads are immortals (minor gods), they can be dangerous or jealous. Their love stories with humans often have unhappy endings.

In ancient Greece, naiads were so admired and respected that many cities were named after them.

O is for Ogre

Every forest should
    post this good advice:
"Befriend an ogre,
    and you pay the price."

Ogres are extremely dangerous, humanoid-looking monsters that patrol woodlands in search of humans to eat. Lazy, scruffy oafs with extendable arms and ear-to-ear mouths, ogres can be smart or stupid, though most would guess the latter. With supernatural strength, they sometimes kill for pure enjoyment.

The term *ogre* may have been the invention of Charles Perrault (1628–1703), the creator of many fairy- and folktales, such as "Cinderella" and "Little Red Riding Hood."

If a human sees an ogre first, the best strategy is to run away as fast as possible. Ogres often appear in fairy tales (such as "Jack and the Beanstalk"), waiting to feed on human beings. Other ogrelike giants include the Norse trolls (large, ugly, evil beings that turn to stone in sunlight) and the Greek Cyclopses ("circle eye," a race of huge one-eyed men).

Today, perhaps the best-known (and best-loved) ogre is Shrek.

Oo

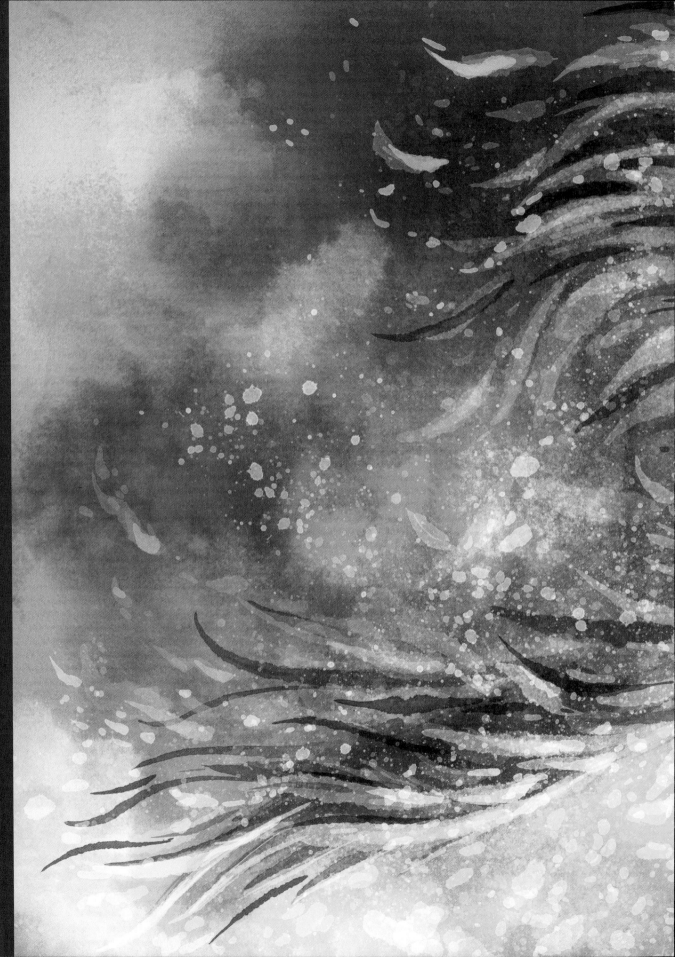

If you believe in rebirth or reincarnation, the mythical story of the Phoenix is one you will enjoy. This brilliantly plumed bird with a tail of gold, purple, scarlet, and blue has a lifespan of five hundred to a thousand years. Toward the end of its life, according to Greek myth, the Phoenix builds a nest of branches and twigs, and then sets it afire, destroying both bird and nest. All that remains are ashes, out of which a new Phoenix is born, and this offspring will then live as long as its predecessor.

In Egypt, the Phoenix is thought of as a stork-like bird; in Greece, it resembles a peacock. Over the centuries, this symbol of rebirth, renewal, and immortality (associated with the sun) has undergone a number of changes in sculptures and paintings around the world, but its captivating story remains.

In 1888, the Phoenix became the official symbol of Atlanta, Georgia, because the city was "reborn" from the ashes after it was burned down in the American Civil War.

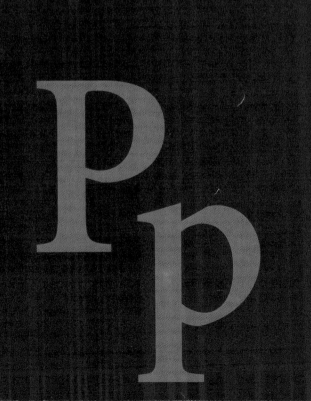

P is for Phoenix

Bird from the ashes,
bird for the ages,
sign of renewal,
symbol courageous.

Q is for Quetzalcoatl

I am snake, I am bird:
I'm the first and last word
that an Aztec used to say
just to pass the time of day.

Quetzalcoatl (pronounced *kweh-tsal-ko-AHT'l*) was the famed ruler of the Aztecs. But the name also refers to the feathered serpent deity, revered in the Aztec religion. His origins are unclear, but this famous bird-snake is related to the dawn, the wind, the planet Venus, arts, crafts, and knowledge. A creature both immortal and human, he can fly, much like a dragon.

Paintings and sculptures of the creature first appeared throughout Mesoamerica (Mexico to northern Costa Rica before the arrival of the Spanish). Considered the inventor of books and the calendar, the bringer of corn (maize) to humans, and the symbol of death and rebirth, Quetzalcoatl is "the lord of the House of dawn." No wonder he was so widely worshipped.

R is for Roc

I hatched from an egg,
    part eagle, part raven.
I live all alone
      on my Roc Mountain haven.

Since monsters are mythical, it is no surprise that the stories of their origins vary widely. Take the Roc, for instance. Here are three tall tales that get taller as time goes on.

1. The Roc originated from a battle between an Indian sky bird and an underground serpent.

2. The Roc was the offspring of an eagle and a raven. One of its dark crimson wings alone was ten feet wide. Shy and introverted, the Roc took revenge on humans who trespassed on Roc Mountain and refused to leave the bird in peace.

3. Having become overheated in the Egyptian desert, the Roc popped out of a gigantic egg, according to archeologist John Avery, who may himself be a myth. Maturing quickly, the Roc flew off to collect ships and buildings to feather its nest. Lifting elephants off the ground and dropping them from great heights must have been child's play for the Roc, which had, Avery claimed, a wingspan of five hundred feet!

Later researchers believed that such outlandish tales were the result of storytellers, who had embellished sightings of eagles and hawks carrying away baby lambs.

R r

Many Native American legends revolve around a skin-walker, a human being able to change into the skin of a coyote or wolf. Skin-walkers fall under the general category of shape shifting, common to many of the world cultures.

Some have suggested that skin-walkers are the "witches of all witches," black magic practitioners who lust for power and wealth, or cause evil willy-nilly. Anyone wishing to become a skin-walker must train for years before being allowed to learn the rituals. Some Navajo believe that the only way one of these creatures can be killed is with a bullet dipped in white ash.

In the extreme, skin-walkers may be observed clawing at the air, speaking in tongues, their faces contorting into animal shapes, though they later return to normal.

Southwest tribes, such as the Navajo, Hopi, and Ute, describe a fascinating and complex history of skin-walkers and their wicked deeds. And beware of a skin-walker who locks eyes with you: a common Navajo belief is he or she can steal your face or be absorbed into your body and steal your thoughts.

S s

S is for Skin-walker

Shifting shape skin-walkers
are the nastiest of stalkers.
Falling under their control,
you may lose your heart and soul.

Tt

Remember the fearsome fiend who ate anyone crossing over his bridge in the Norwegian fairy tale "Three Billy Goats Gruff"? That nasty fellow was a troll, a supernatural being that appears often in Scandinavian mythology. Like elves and fairies, trolls dwell in rocks, mountains, and caves, and they are nasty to humans.

Trolls are often described as old though extremely strong and dim-witted. In fact, they may look like you or me, but they rarely go near humans. Early trolls were giants, but dwarf trolls began to appear in later folktales. They hate sunlight, which can turn them to stone. What really frightens them is lightning, and what annoys them is the constant ringing of church bells (hence, they keep their distance from humans).

The rise of Christianity transformed trolls from folklore characters to demons, monstrous and deadly. But once the tourist industry discovered trolls, they changed once again—from characters that were frightening to dolls that are lovable, cute, and even lucky. Still, for safety's sake, Scandinavians usually avoid going into forests after dark.

T is for Troll

Trolls are trouble.
It's well known
you shouldn't walk
in the woods alone!

U is for Unicorn

Ancient forests can leave you spellbound
when a unicorn's horsing around.
If your paths haven't crossed,
it may be that she's lost,
but the fact is she's never been found.

U u

This legendary creature of grace and beauty is portrayed as a white horse with a goat's beard, though descriptions vary. Its most remarkable feature is the stunning, pointed spiral horn protruding from its forehead. In early Europe, many so-called unicorn horns were bought and sold out of "cabinets of curiosities" by hucksters eager to make a quick franc or mark. In reality the horns were those of the narwhal, a medium-sized toothed whale that lives year-round in the Arctic.

Many believe the unicorn has magical powers to cleanse poisoned water and to heal sickness. It is said that the best way to hunt a unicorn is to set a young girl in the forest. The unicorn's natural shyness will be overcome and it cannot help but be attracted by something as innocent and pure as a young female.

The desire to capture the real thing has led to numerous hoaxes, including burying horse bones, digging them up, and identifying them as unicorn remains. If two-pronged African antelopes, such as the oryx and the eland, were seen in profile, they were sometimes mistaken for unicorns.

V is for Vampire

I looked in the mirror
late one night,
the mirror cracked up
at my overbite!

A vampire is a creature of folklore that lives by feeding on the blood of either the undead or living persons. They did not become popular until the eighteenth century when superstitions spread across Europe. And one man, Bram Stoker, lifted the vampire to new heights (or depths) with his 1897 novel, *Dracula*. With his long fangs, Dracula bit his victims on the neck and drank their blood. Result? They became vampires, too.

How else does one become a vampire? Traditions differ in time and place, but in Chinese and Slavic lore, any corpse that is jumped over by an animal, say a dog or cat, is thought to be vulnerable. Likewise, a person with a wound untreated with boiling water is considered to be a potential member of the undead.

Vampires have no reflections in the mirror, nor do they cast any shadows. Various ways to repel, if not defeat, them include: the use of holy water, rosaries, crucifixes, garlic, a wooden stake, or by allowing sunlight to fall upon them.

Their popularity has grown enormously through books, television shows, and movies such as *Buffy the Vampire Slayer* and Stephanie Meyer's Twilight series.

V v

Legends say that a werewolf, quite human-looking in daylight, is transformed into a wolflike creature under a full moon. The technical term for such a being is a lycanthrope. In other cultures, animals popular to a region have metamorphosed into were-dogs, -bears, -boars, -jaguars, -hyenas, -tigers, and so forth.

Various theories are cited for how someone becomes a werewolf such as being cursed, being bitten by a werewolf, or eating poisoned herbs. In appearance, werewolves may have unibrows, different-colored eyes, curved fingernails, or a bright red birthmark (the "mark of Cain"), but most prominently, very hairy skin. It is also said that many werewolves are sorcerers who will themselves into changing into wolves.

Feared for its ravenous appetite and superhuman strength, a werewolf will devour whole herds of livestock or steal children from their beds. They are depicted as immune to harm caused by ordinary weapons, but as first suggested in films, they are said to be vulnerable to silver objects, like a silver bullet or blade.

W is for Werewolf

Each morning I begin
        with clean, smooth-shaven skin,
    but night brings out my weird
        and thick full-body beard.

X

In a time before time, as myths begin, the Emperor Yan was defeated by the Yellow Emperor, the father of Chinese civilization. During the battle, one of Yan's followers, a nameless giant, challenged the Yellow Emperor to a duel. The two fought viciously with axe and sword. The Emperor with one last blow struck the giant, whose head rolled to the edge of the mountain and down with a deafening roar.

This would be the end of the story for any normal human being. But the dead giant, known as Xing Tian, was supposedly able to regenerate himself. He crawled around looking for his head. From that time on, the headless giant had eyes in his chest, and a mouth on his navel.

Xing Tian means "the punished one," or "he who was punished by heaven," and the mere sight of him was enough to haunt the dreams of onlookers. Armed with a shield and an axe, he could sense any movement nearby. This rampaging monster attacked anyone or anything in his way, and would never give up.

X is for Xing Tian

Here's a giant without a head,
so of course he must be dead.
But if you meet him eye to eye,
this cruel beast will never say die.

Yy

Like Bigfoot in the United States, the major monster of the Himalayas is the mysterious Yeti, a legend that got started in the nineteenth century. First named in 1921, it's also known as the Abominable Snowman, and its existence is forever a part of the Tibetan and Nepalese mountains. The Tibetan name *yeti* is a combination of "rocky" and "bear," condensed from the Sherpa word, *yeh-teh*.

The descriptions of Yeti are varied and wild: a huge, naked apelike creature; woolly brown- or white-haired; sharp teeth; long arms; no tail; and strong enough to wrestle a bear. As with Bigfoot, numerous amateur expeditions over the years have found large footprints and hairs. A Nepalese monastery has even put a so-called Yeti scalp on display.

In 2011 Russian enthusiasts claimed to have "considerable evidence" of the creature's existence. But other more reliable observers disputed this boast, saying it was most likely made to generate publicity and tourism. The likelihood is that the Yeti footprints are those of a brown bear or an Asiatic black bear, but you would probably be wise not to say so out loud. True believers in the Abominable Snowman hate being contradicted.

Y is for Yeti

Bigfoot's relative, some say, is
    hiding out in the Himalayas.
Known by everyone as Yeti,
    he's probably a bear (but not a teddy).

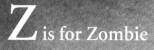

Z is for Zombie

A zombie looks so strange!
He's undergone a change
so frightful that instead
of living he's "undead."

Let's begin with a true statement: few scientists really believe in the "undead." "Acting like a zombie" is sometimes used to describe people under hypnosis who lack all self-awareness but are still able to respond to stimuli. True zombies, the frightening creatures of fiction, folklore, and contemporary films, are said to have an enormous appetite for human flesh.

Vodou, a Haitian creole word (also Voodoo, Vodun, or Vodoun), originated in West Africa in the early nineteenth century. According to Vodou, a dead person can be brought back to life as a zombie by a *bokor* (sorcerer) who takes command of the deceased's will. Others believe that zombies are reanimated but soulless corpses, such as those seen in Western pop culture.

The fascination with zombies has never been more widespread than it is today as a sub-genre of horror and fantasy. They can be seen in Michael Jackson's "Thriller" music video, comics, video games, television shows, and movies.

Of all the beasts in and outside this book, zombies are the creatures most closely associated with doomsday and the end of the world.

Zz

For Kelly and Scott

JPL

—•—

For Kiernan, Morris, Kendrick, and Sheila

GK

Sleeping Bear Press
315 E. Eisenhower Parkway, Suite 200
Ann Arbor, MI 48108
www.sleepingbearpress.com

Printed and bound in the United States.

10 9 8 7 6 5 4 3 2 1

Library of Congress Cataloging-in-Publication Data

Lewis, J. Patrick.
M is for monster : a fantastic creatures alphabet / written by J. Patrick Lewis ;
ilustrated by Gerald Kelley.
pages cm.
ISBN 978-1-58536-818-1
1. Monsters–Juvenile literature. 2. Alphabet–Juvenile literature. I. Title.
GR825.L48 2014
001.944–dc23
2013050682